MEMORIES OF THE MAN WITH 9 LIVES

Gail Holditch Adams

America Star Books
Frederick, Maryland

Softcover 9781681227283
PUBLISHED BY AMERICA STAR BOOKS, LLLP
www.americastarbooks.pub
Frederick, Maryland

TABLE OF CONTENTS

PROLOGUE

I was married to the man who had 9 plus lives. His name was Bud/Boyd. The stories you will read are all true and compiled over the 45 years that we were married. My name is Gail.

CHAPTER ONE

THE CAMPFIRE

I recall one of the many times that Bud decided to have a camp fire. When it wouldn't catch fire, he poured the gasoline to it. And, when that didn't seem to catch a spark, he would approach the awaiting bundle of kindling and wood and attempt to pour on 'just a little more gasoline—why not empty the container, he would say, as he emptied it. And, just as he approached the pile of wood with his lighter all aflame, the wood exploded, scorching his eyebrows, and front of his hair, not to mention the front of his clothes. He then turned to our daughter-in-law with charred eyebrows and said, "Don't tell Gail."

CAMPFIRE TWO

There was another time when he had his wood and kindling all set for the match—and gas. He doused the entire thing, saturating every square inch of wood, making sure that good results would come about. He never had a match, but would bend over to use his lighter. When the wood didn't catch fire, he thought it a splendid idea to pour more gasoline over it, (obviously not learning a lesson from the other thousand times he did this stunt). He stepped back, waiting for the fire to burst upward from the tinder. He waited the allotted time (his time) which amounted to a tenth of a second and approached it again with his gas can. He stood with a cigarette in his mouth, and tipping the container he watched as the gas poured out the spout and onto the awaiting kindling. The wood having a delayed reaction from the first two pours, exploded! The flames ran up the gas to the container he was holding. His hand got stuck in the handle and he flung the container as far as he could. It left a burn mark a good 20 yards on the grass and he suffered some weeks with burns to his hands.

THE OLD TRUCK

There was the time Bud traded an old camera for a ½ ton truck. The day after he bought it, it would not start. (Is it any wonder? A truck for a camera?) With a cigarette in his mouth he fetched an old piece of garden hose and siphoned some gas from the tank, then proceeded to pour the gas over the carburetor and had me try and start the truck. The sparks flew, and he let go of the hose, sending gasoline all down the front of him and into the shorts he was wearing at the time. The old truck never did get out of the driveway.

THE LANTERN

One time we were camping with our son and daughter-in-law. As we were preparing to leave for home, Bud noticed a lantern hanging from a branch on the empty lot across from us.

"Oh, look over there," he said pointing to the empty lot with the attached lantern hanging listlessly. "I bet they forgot it," he said as he aimed in that direction.

"Bud, someone would not leave something behind if it was in good working order," I said.

"Gail! No, they just forgot it! There is nothing wrong with it! You'll see."

With that, he took the lantern home. He put it in the shed, and the next weekend our son and wife were visiting and Bud decided it was a good time to try out the lantern. Off he went to the shed to retrieve the lantern and after filling it with fuel he came into the house and placed it on the kitchen counter. He was about to light it, when I told him that there was no way he was going to light that thing in the house, the 'thing' was leaking fuel faster than water being soaked up in the desert. He took it outside mumbling all the way as fuel was leaking all down his arms. We watched from the window as he flicked his lighter, lit the awaiting cigarette hanging from his mouth, then proceeded to lift the glass cover and light the wick. The flames shot out, all over the lamp, and down his arms, setting him on fire. He quickly put his hands in between his legs trying to put the flames out. As his pants smoldered, we all stood in the window watching.

QUITTING SMOKING

Bud would quit smoking, no doubt due to a promise he made to me when he wanted to buy something—big. But he continued to smoke behind my back. One day I just happened to look out the kitchen window to see smoke coming from the open door of the shed.

I opened the kitchen door and shouted, "Are you smoking?" With that, he jumped, hit his head on the top of the shed, which jarred his hearing aids out of his ears and into the open container of garbage. The next day, he was looking for his hearing aids, only to realize where they might be. Of course, garbage day had come and gone, taking his three thousand dollar hearing aids with the rest of the garbage.

QUITTING SMOKING, TWO

Then there was another time, that Bud had quit smoking—again, and I happened to come home from work (I worked only blocks away from home) to change my uniform as my pen had leaked ink. When I came in the house, I yelled that I was home, but, having no hearing aids in, he did not hear, and I ran downstairs to get a new uniform from the laundry room. I passed by the open door of the washroom which was next to the laundry room and he was at the moment wiping himself. He had the soiled paper in one hand, and a cigarette in the other. When he saw me, he wasn't quite sure which was heading for his mouth and which was heading for the toilet.

FASTEETH DENTURE POWDER

There was the time when my parents were staying overnight with us before leaving for Florida. Bud got up to leave for work, and was trying to be as quiet as he could be. He left the house, then had a second thought, thinking that when he came home that night, he would be all smelling from sweat (he worked on construction). So he came back in to put on some after bath powder. He did not want to put a light on and disturb our guests. He knew where everything was in his own medicine cabinet, so he reached in, grabbed the container of what he thought was bath powder. He opened up his pants, and poured some in, front and back. He lifted his shirt and splashed some around there. Off to work he went. That night, he came home and immediately headed for the bathroom. He then opened the door slightly to call me. I went to see what the problem was only to find him standing there with all his clothes stuck to his privates and other bits and pieces of flesh. He had grabbed his container of 'Fast Teeth" a powder used for false teeth to hold them in. Once the powder hits any moisture, it turns to paste, a sticky holding paste similar to super glue.

PROPANE

One time we were driving in our Motor Home (an old one) over the Ambassador Bridge going into the States. I said, "Bud, I smell propane."

"Gail! It's the shitter. I didn't empty it from the last time." (Last year's holiday—or the one before that).

"Oh," I said.

When the smell became stronger, I mentioned my thoughts on the matter again. He never spoke until we crossed over into the States when he pulled over to check, 'just in case'. The valve to the propane tanks underneath the Motor Home was wide open and pouring out propane.

PROPANE TWO

And, there is another propane story I must add. We had another Motor home, second hand, with a few missing items—like lots. It was both gas and propane operated. We filled up the tanks, plus filled our barbecue tanks for home and the 'home in the woods' that we had. We had besides these cylinders of propane, a huge one, a 100 lb one. We filled it, too. But, being that we could not have it stand, as it was too tall, Bud placed it along the floor in the Motor Home. Which we found out later, that you should never lie one down on its side. He was smoking, and cleaning the windows inside the van. I came out with a bundle of food to put in the refrigerator. I smelt propane. When I mentioned my concerns (again) he informed me that it was the 'shitter'. I said I didn't think so, it smelt like propane. He got a little ticked off with my suspicions, and continued to smoke and clean the windows, furthering himself down inside the motor home to clean the side windows. When I came back with another load for the refrigerator, I now heard hissing, quite loud, plus the smell of propane very strong. I again mentioned the smell, and he again informed me it was the 'shitter'. I asked him then how come I hear hissing.

Hissing, he asked? With that, he quickly left the motor home and headed to the back yard, butting his smoke out, and sitting himself down on a chair due to feeling weak. He was as white as a ghost.

TRAILER PASSING THE CAR

I recall one time, we were heading out to Prince Edward Island. I was driving, and we were towing a small little trailer with some goodies we were taking down there. We had a cottage there where we spent the summer. I was driving and heard a noise. I asked him what he thought the noise was. He said it was nothing. "Well, if it is nothing," I said, "then why was our trailer passing us?"

He had forgotten to hook the trailer onto the hitch, it was only attached with the chains. The trailer then smashed into the back end of the car, and thank goodness, it was the trailer that took the brunt of the crash as the hitch buried itself so deep into the wall of the trailer. I had to drive the car forward slowly while Bud lifted until we were free of the trailer.

Then as we were driving through Montreal, Quebec, towing the trailer, that had no brakes, Bud didn't think we needed them on a small trailer. People were passing us and telling us that our trailer was flying about. Bud said it was nothing. I thought the trailer would flip over, and my nerves got the best of me. My mouth must have been flopping the entire time as Bud was driving. By the time we got to the outskirts of Montreal, the brakes were smoking on our vehicle and they ceased up.

CANADIAN TIRE

One time we had to put the Motor Home into the garage, (Canadian Tire) to be looked at. Bud was in the garage section waiting for them to do something. He got tired of waiting and decided to light a smoke. He perched himself on the back bumper of the Motor Home. The mechanic came along and unaware that Bud was sitting on the back, proceeded to hoist the vehicle up as high as it would go. Bud never said a word and thought it would be a change of scenery from up above. After he finished his smoke, he got bored, and looked down and thought that didn't seem that far down, so he jumped,(I might add, he was around 80 at the time). Of course, everyone came running, including some of the staff from inside the store. He hurt himself, but not to the extent that required hospitalization.

The next time we were passing by we noticed a large sign hanging at the entrance of the garage that read, 'Employees Only'.

ROTORS

There was the time we went to Mexico, in the old Motor Home that should not have left the driveway of our home, let alone, Canada. We got as far as the border in Texas, when I thought I heard a noise. It was nothing, he said. But, I refused to enter Mexico without checking it out. To satisfy me, we went to a garage to see what the noise was that I had heard. The mechanic said that the rotors were paper thin (not to mention what the brake pads were like) and we wouldn't have gotten too far before we would have had serious trouble. Bud said that we could still drive years before we had trouble. The mechanic heard Bud and gave him the rotors and brake pads to keep as a reminder. And, I let Bud know in not too many words my thoughts on the matter.

~~

LEAVING ME BEHIND

There was the time we stopped for gas, somewhere between Ontario and Mexico. I took advantage of the opportunity to use the washroom in the gas station. When I was in there, I decided to buy some pop, chips and a couple of chocolate bars. When I came out, Bud was driving off! I hung my purse around my neck and went running. My purse was flying about and I was yelling. Of course, he could not hear, even when he had hearing aids in. As he picked up speed to exit the service road and enter the thruway, I too, picked up speed. It reminded me of the cartoons of the Road Runner. Bud happened to look in his side mirror for on-coming traffic, and was horrified to see that the on-coming traffic just happened to be me, with my purse flying about my neck! My mouth was flopping, and by the time I settled into my seat, he informed me that when I said I was going to the washroom, he thought the washroom I was going to was the one in the Motor Home.

By the way, this same scene happened, twice!

~~

MEXICO

While in Mexico, we decided to park (for free) on the beach. We waited until all the beach traffic had left and we found ourselves a nice spot, facing out, in case we had to leave quickly. Before going to bed, Bud informed me that just in case I heard something, I was to let him know. We closed the curtain separating us from the front of the motor home, hence giving us privacy. He left the keys in the ignition, 'just in case', he had said. I was sleeping in the upper berth, above the driver's seat, and he was sleeping on the table which converted to a bed. During the night, I was awakened to several vehicles with full beam headlights shining on us, directly at the front of our Motor Home. I gingerly crept down, and whispered in Bud's ear. Of course he didn't hear me. I then shook him, trying to arouse him. He woke, and I put my fingers to my lips to say, 'shush'. Of course that didn't work. He pulled himself to a sitting position on the edge of the bed, and said, aloud, (he had to speak loud enough to hear himself). "What's wrong?" he asked.

I put my fingers to my lips again, to say shush, and then whispered right into his ear canal, "There is someone outside."

"What?"

"I said, there is someone outside!" I again whispered taking it a few degrees higher and pushing my mouth a little further into his ear canal.

"Wait, I can't hear you. Wait until I find my hearing aids."

"Shush."

"What?"

"I said, there is someone outside our motorhome," I said pointing outside, and nearly freaking out.

He started to look through the bed for his hearing aids, but found instead his teeth and put them in.

"Wait, I have to go to the bathroom. Tell me when I get back. Can you look for my hearing aids?" he said loudly as he made his way down the hall to the washroom.

In the meantime, I am nearly having a bird, as more vehicles were arriving. I could visualize them circling our motorhome. My mind started going, thinking that they plan on having a party, with us as their party. My blood pressure I am sure had developed an all-time high without the stroke.

"I found your hearing aids, here," I whispered as I handed them to him.

"What are you whispering about?" he asked as he inserted them in his ears. Then started to fine tune them. The aids were whistling away at their highest decibel while he turned them down.

"There are a bunch of cars outside, and I hear a lot of voices," I said.

With that, his eyes popped out, and as he slid himself down the hall, toward the driver's seat, he asked, "Why didn't you wake me up earlier?" He started the Motor Home from under the curtain and drove out as fast as he could.

FALSE TEETH

One time we went for a drive in the Motor Home. He was driving and his teeth were bothering him, so he took them out and put them between his legs. Several hours later we decided to stop for a coffee at Tim Hortons. He parked across the road from Tims, which was on a main highway. We went into the donut shop, used their bathroom and got coffee and donuts to go. A mile or so down the road, we started into the donuts. Bud started hunting all over for his teeth. He felt his shirt pockets, then checked the bins on the door, in the console, and felt his pants pockets, no teeth. THEN, a light went off. He recalled putting them between his legs. Perhaps they slid out when we stopped for coffee, he suggested. I get myself positioned to look all over the floor while he is driving, and even looked under his foot which was propped on the gas pedal. No teeth. We turned around and headed back to where we had stopped. Sure enough, there were his teeth! The bottom plate was intact and the tops, well, let me say this, it was hard to distinguish that they had ever been an upper plate. All there was left were several loose teeth, and bits and pieces of pink plate. The teeth must have slipped under the Motor Home and when we left we drove over them.

HEARING AIDS, TWO

On the same road trip above, we thought we would look for vacant land, something that always interested us. We saw a for sale sign which led us miles down a country road. We walked the entire property, which consisted of several acres. Bud thought it a good time to go to the bathroom. While he was doing his business, his one hearing aid was bothering him, so he took it out and placed it, he thought, in his shirt pocket. We left that property, and went miles down the road, when he discovered he had lost his hearing aid. Back we drove, and walked the land, but with the dead grass looking the same as his hearing aid, we placed another mark on the wall and filed it under the heading, 'Lost hearing aids'. That file sits alongside the file, "Lost teeth', and next to that, 'lost keys'.

MOTORCYCLE

Then there were the three motorcycle accidents that he was involved in, one included me.

~~

Three or four car accidents. One involving him hitting the behind of the car in front, sending the guys gas tank flying. The guy was so mad at Bud because he had just filled up his gas tank.

~~

Another time he didn't clean the frost off of his windshield. It was one of those days when there was white frost everywhere. Everything was white, and he could not tell where the roads crossed, so continued on into a hydro pole, and taking it down.

~~

FALLING 48 FEET

And the time he fell down off the climbing crane he was working on. He was a Crane Operator. He fell 48 ft. He spent one year total downtime.

While he was in a body cast, from below the knees up to under his armpits, I brought him home from the hospital as I thought the change of scenery would be good for him. I set up a hospital bed in the front room so that he could watch the television and see the traffic out front. I was working. I worked midnight shift and our son was there for his needs during the night. I recall on one occasion coming home in the morning, and he had worked himself off the bed and was in a standing position. He said he was bored. He was one solid hunk of plaster, reminded me of a huge fire hydrant, without the hose. It took all my strength between him and me to get him back into the bed. He couldn't bend, and had to hold the monkey bars while I lifted a ton of cast, plus him, into the bed. I threatened him with his life that time!

THE FREEZER

There was the time we bought a freezer. Well, it was one we didn't need. Somehow the fuse was switched off by someone (no names mentioned) who was fixing the dishwasher and forgot to return it to its normal state. I went to go into the freezer and found it was all defrosting. Off we went to buy another. After purchasing one, we were too cheap to use the convenient delivery service of the store, and decided we would bring it home ourselves. We laid the car seats down, and slid the freezer in. Home we came. Now, the freezer was going down a long flight of stairs. He thought it a good idea, to tie a rope around my waist and he stood down the stairs holding it at the bottom preventing it from sliding down the steps taking him with it. My job he told me, was to hold tightly to the frame around the door. Well, we gently slid the thing down, but thought after how foolish we both were.

CHEATER WASHROOM

We had a home that had a 'cheater washroom'. During the night I was sitting on the throne, when I heard him stirring and making his way to the washroom.

"I'm in here," I said.

I heard him continuing to come.

"I am in here," I now said much louder.

And he is still making his way into my privacy.

Into the bathroom he came, all prepared to use the toilet immediately, I hollered, again.

Of course, him being stone deaf, did not hear, and as he stood towering above me about to use the toilet, while I was still sitting, I let one bellow out of me and it scared the life out of him.

~~

CHAPTER TWO

FIRE (NOT CAMP FIRE)

We had a cottage in Prince Edward Island, as I have mentioned somewhere above. We also had a Bunkie that sat on the lot.

I was in the cottage, and saw Bud's partially bald head passing by the window. I thought nothing of it. But, when I saw him passing back and forth, it caused a stir within me of what was going on. I got up to look. He was carrying very carefully—for fear of losing a drop—a soup can (tomato) filled with water to the back of the house. I wondered what he was doing. Our well sat near the front of the house, at the side. He was coming from the well. I thought to myself, this must be important.

Shortly after that trip he was making, on his return, he ran into the house to tell me that the Bunkie was on fire! I ran and grabbed some big pots, filled them with water and headed out to the Bunkie. Yes, indeed it was on fire. He had already removed the mattress that was on fire by then, and a few other items that he must have prided—like his smokes. I quickly put the fire out. I asked him why he was going back and forth to the well with a soup can of water. "Well, how else was I supposed to put the fire out?" He angrily said.

"But why didn't you use the garden hose that is lying here?" I asked pointing to the hose.

"I didn't see it," was his short reply.

"How did the fire start?" I questioned, waiting for that most exciting answer.

"Well, I saw a few threads hanging from the mattress and thought I could just burn them off with my lighter," he said.

"I see," I said.

DRIVING

There were numerous times that when I would be driving, he would tell me to pass the slow transport or farm tractor that was ahead of us, on a steep hill, with the solid line. "You can make it, just drive the thing (well, there were a few words before the word, 'thing')!

BUD GETTING SCOLDED...BY ME

Even when he was ill in his last days of life, I took him to the hospital for his check up with the Respiratory Specialist. My sister came with me to help as Bud was now in a wheelchair, plus two cylinders of oxygen. After the visit to the doctor, I told my sister to wait in the lobby and I would go and get the car, which was miles away, it felt. As I drove slowly up to find a spot by the front door, Bud happened to see me pass by. He took off wheeling himself heading rapidly to the revolving doors. My sister had to get up from her chair (she is now getting elderly herself) and grab her bag, plus the empty oxygen tank, and by the time she sorted herself out, he was gone, making his way around in the revolving doors. They move slowly, and my sister is now caught on the other side standing in line waiting for a slot to come around. She is yelling at him from the other side of the doors. Bud is now out the door, and wheeling himself like he was going to the circus! I could not get a spot close so was parked about 10 car lengths away from the front door, and as I got out of my car, I noticed Bud flying down the ramp that led to the main street where cars were parked along the side of the street and he would be presenting himself to unaware drivers.

As I began running I am screaming for someone to grab hold of him. I could hear my sister, who is still caught in the revolving doors, yelling. When I caught up to him, I was fuming! He had this grin on his face that he got when he pulled a fast one on me or someone! He would put this grin on when he knew he had gotten my goat. He surely did! More than my goat! I angrily slapped his knee and told him never to do that again! Just then, two men came along, saw me slapping a man that was bald (due to Chemo), elderly (he was 11 years my senior) white (due to cancer), oxygen tube going into his nose (Shortness of breath) swollen legs and feet (due to Congestive heart failure) with only socks on (unable to put shoes on).

"You can't do that!" the two men said to me as they watched me slap his knee.

I felt like a nickel, and by now my sister has caught up to him and said she was so mad she could hit him over the head with the empty oxygen tank. I am now feeling guilty and looked around to see if anyone caught the action on their phone—I could see this on the evening news.

"I'll buy you an ice cream," I said, feeling like a heel. This was a treat to him being a diabetic.

He smiled, then he turned to look at me and said, "She pushed me."

"He doesn't deserve an ice cream!" my sister cried, with tears of anger flowing down her cheeks.

Bud got his ice cream, and my sister didn't talk to us the rest of the night.

BUD'S PURCHASES

There was the time he came home from work in Toronto. We lived in Newmarket at the time. He informed me that there was this Motor Home that I had to see. "Gail! I don't want to buy it, I just want you to look at it," he said in passing.

"Bud, we can't afford a Motor Home, we can't even afford a better car. We both commute over an hours' drive each way to work, and need a car more than we need a Motor Home!" I said.

Weeks went by, and not a day passed that he didn't mention the Motor Home to me. Then, one Sunday, my mother and I were going past that very same spot that the Motor Home rested in, a Trailer Sales yard. I decided to stop in, and peek in the windows, the least I could do, I thought. As I was standing on tippy-toes, casting my eyes as far as I could, a man approached me and told me it was sold.

"Oh, isn't that a shame. My husband had his eyes on this," I said with a smile.

"Well, let me make sure that it is sold. Come into the office, and I will look." As he opened the Sales book, he ran his fingers down the names of those that had purchased a vehicle from them. As his finger ran down the column, I happen to notice Bud's signature! I was horrified! He paid over 10 thousand dollars, CASH! I am sure my tires never touched pavement all the way home! He was out in the yard with our little toy dog when he saw me coming. It must have been the look on my face that he recognized, and he picked up our little dog and headed into the house.

I had to run to the bank and take money from one account to cover the cheque he wrote. I was not impressed!

CAN'T BREATHE

There was the time when he was on oxygen, and he was in bed. I must have tangled up the long tubing that stretched down the hall to the bedroom when vacuuming. I was in the front room with our son and daughter-in-law and he said in a faint voice, "I can't breathe."

I looked at the oxygen machine and it was running, and I said, "It is working." But, then thought I best check the machine and tubing. Sure enough there was a kink in the tube. I corrected it.

"We then heard a faint voice saying, "I can breathe now."
We all felt like heels.

HOUSE BUYING...WITHOUT ME

Then there was the time he got his eye on a house. I didn't care for it, in fact, I hated it. I had to go to a funeral, and I just had a 'funny feeling' that he might just do something I would not be happy with. When I came home, he informed me he bought the house, and we then had to put our own home up for sale to cover the down payment for the other house. We did not sell in time, so had to take a bridge loan out. I think you can gather my feelings on the matter.

It was this house that I hated that was later condemned due to the wiring being unsafe. The basement flooded. It was also this house that he had the accident at work, falling 48 ft. In fact it was the day after we moved in.

And it was this house that we bought a boat, (yes another boat) a big one, and Bud had to take it from dry dock in Bracebridge, Ontario, and onto the awaiting trailer. It was a Sunday, and Bud asked my Dad to help him. My Dad really did not want to do this on a Sunday. But, he went as well as our young son. Bud was at the wench, (he being a Hoisting Engineer) and our son and my Dad were at the hook, making sure it was taunt. Bud had some odd feeling, so told our son to go and stand somewhere else. With no fault of Bud's, the hook straightened out, crashing into my dad's forehead. He was wearing glasses at the time, and it was a 2 thousand pound thrust that hit him in the forehead. He did survive that, but lost one eye and most of the vision in the other.

REAL ESTATE

Then there was the time that I went to Church with my mother. We had our house up for sale (no not the house mentioned above, this is another one, (one of the 15 that we bought and sold). Apparently, the Realtor phoned, and Bud didn't have his hearing aids in, so did not hear it. The realtor then figured we were not home and came with new clients to show the home. Bud was laying on the floor watching television. He didn't have his teeth in, they were somewhere, always somewhere but in his mouth, and he wasn't dressed appropriately for entertaining guests. He just had on his underwear, the long white jobs with the trap door that he hated doing up because he always had to undo it. Well, they rang the doorbell and of course he did not hear it and in they came. The realtor came into the front room to show it, and here Bud was on the floor, he looked up, saw people (all female) standing there in the doorway staring at him. He scrambled to his feet, went in search of his teeth and (no doubt a smoke), which were laying on the kitchen counter. As he dodged around in his long whites with his behind hanging out, the realtor suggested they start with the bedrooms upstairs first.

BOAT AUCTION

There was the time Bud bought a boat. Well, actually he bought 6 boats at an auction. The one boat had an outboard motor that did not run. He towed the boat with attached motor to a mechanic to be fixed. The next day I came home from work and he asked if I was ready to go for a ride. I asked him was the motor fixed already. He said, "Sure."

But apparently the mechanic never got around to checking it out. Bud got impatient and decided he didn't really need it fixed, which I did not know.

Off we went to a lake near the village where we lived. He backed the boat trailer into the water, until the water was near the front seat of the Jeep. He nearly had to be towed out. He got out of that mess and went and parked the Jeep, and off we went. A crowd had now gathered on the dock to watch us. I guess after the near fiasco of backing the Jeep into the lake, they thought this might be worthwhile watching. Bud dropped the motor down into the water and it sunk into the deep sand below, like quicksand it was. He tried to get it loosened, and finally had to jump into the water and lift from the bottom while I lifted from the top. We got out of that, and now we were set to go boating. I paddled out into deep water and he then dropped the motor, again. After about a thousand tries, it ignited and off we went. I settled into the seat, and Bud started waving at the passing boats, he was now captain! He even waved at the crowd that was starting to disperse at the dock. I suggested we not go out too far as we didn't know the motor or the lake.

"It is fine, nothing wrong with the motor. It is just fine!" he said.

We motored way out and around the bend in the lake, then smoke started pouring out from the motor. It sputtered and spit and then stopped. I forgot to mention that we only had one paddle. Bud said we didn't need another. I paddled and paddled until a fine gentleman with a tiny wee boat towed us to shore to a mechanic. The mechanics wife drove Bud around to the head of the lake where our Jeep was and I went with the mechanic in the boat. He kept trying to start the motor, and it caught, but only until we got way out in the lake. He asked where my other paddle was, and I said we only had the one. What do you talk about in the quietness of the lake, with a stranger? I asked how come they landed way out here in the country. He said he had had a very bad heart attack and the doctor suggested a nice quiet atmosphere. Here I am sitting while he was paddling like mad, and I suggested that it was my turn to take the paddle. I wasn't about to be out in the lake with someone having a heart attack, all because of us!

~~

BOAT STORY—TWO

Another one of our boat stories. We bought a little tiny dory, the small boat that you tow behind a larger boat. We had a little 3 horsepower motor. At the time we were in Prince Edward Island at our cottage. There was a river out front which took you out to the ocean. Again, we decided to take a nice boat ride, just in the river.

We cast off, and I suggested that we not go out far, as we did not know the motor. We had just bought it, cheap. I worry too much, Bud said. As we pushed off, Bud started to pull the cord on the motor. After several tries, there was a pile of water coming up and over my ankles. I said we should go back to the dock, and empty the water out. Don't worry, as soon as the motor starts, the water will be sucked out, he said. But the longer he tried to start the motor, the more water was coming in. I now am taking my hands and cupping the water out. We got way out, and nearing the entrance into the ocean, he now was getting a little frightened, and we headed quickly back to shore. We got to shore, (when the water was ¼ way up the sides of the boat) and he discovered that he hadn't put the plug in.

BOAT STORY—THREE

There was another boat story when we were way up north and thought it would be nice to have a boat so we bought a rubber dingy at a garage sale.

"We should check for leaks before we go out in it," I suggested.

"It will be fine," he said.

Off we went into a lake up north, and after we left shore the air started leaking out. By the time we got turned around and headed for shore, we were nearly swimming. Walking ashore, we left the pile of rubber on the side of the shore.

~~

BOAT STORY—FOUR

Another time, shortly after we bought the fiberglass dory, the one that the plug didn't get plugged in, we went on holidays up north. We dropped the boat into a lake and with the small 3 horsepower motor and off we went. The name of the lake was called, 'Long Lake'. Well, we went the length of it, and the motor died. We again had only one paddle, and with the two of us taking turns, we were exhausted as the wind was against us, with each forward move, we moved twice back. Eventually I went into shore, and left him and our little dog in the boat while I got out and got hold of the rope and towed it manually up the lake keeping close to the shore line. I passed by areas where you can see where animals come down for a drink of water, (all sorts of animals, bears included were being visualized in my mind). I felt like, Humphrey Bogart, in 'African Queen'.

AND, YET ANOTHER BOAT STORY

One of the boats that we bought at an auction, we kept. It was a fair size. When we sold the farm and were moving to London, which was hundreds of miles away, Bud wanted to bring the boat, too. He decided to tow it with the Motor Home. It was winter, and the boat was filled with snow. He nearly blew the motor out of the old Motor Home due to he was not only towing the boat filled with snow, but he had forgotten to pull the plug when he stored it and it filled with water which turned to solid ice.

~~

FISHING

Then there was the time we went fishing with a number of people. We had a small boat. It was the beginning of fishing season, and the weather was a mite cold. I made sure I dressed for the occasion. I suggested to Bud that he too, dress for it. He would be fine, he assured me. I asked if he had 2 (TWO) paddles. He would get them, he said. Away we went fishing. We got out in the middle of the lake, and yes, we had two paddles, but the motor stopped working. Bud was cold, he said, and asked if he could have one of my jackets, or sweater, or anything. He was nearly shaking from the cold. Then, of course, he was so chilled that he then had to pee. Well, he wasn't that stable on his feet and he tried to stand in the tiny boat so that he could pee over the side of the boat. I shifted to one side of the boat, and he became very wobbly and nearly fell which would dump the boat and us. He didn't know what to do, so he got down on his knees and tried to hang his what-cha-ma-call-it over the edge of the boat. Well, it didn't reach, (which I being a nurse could have told him) and he ended up peeing in the boat. I then had to sit with my feet hanging over the edge of the boat as we headed home. I don't think we even got our fishing lines in the water that time.

RING

There was the time I bought him a solid gold ring for his birthday. How he loved rings! The very next day, he and I were travelling down the main highway leading into Toronto. We had separate cars, and as he passed me, he held his hand out the window to show off his ring. Somehow the ring slipped off and was caught up with the traffic behind us. We never did go back to look for it.

RING-TWO

Then there was another time, we owned a Hotel. Bud was making homemade hamburger patties. While he was mixing the meat, his ring came off, unnoticed by him. Someone got a mouthful of ring in their hamburger. No one said a word

RESTAURANT BUSINESS

Speaking of Hotels. We owned a restaurant with a motel, too. Well, that was something! Neither of us knew the first thing about cooking, or the job of waitressing. We tossed a coin, which one was going to cook and which one was going to be the waitress. I lost and ended up in the hot kitchen. We had no air conditioning in the kitchen, only the dining room had it. We had no money and had to borrow some from my parents to put in the till so that we could make change. To save money, I did all the laundry and cleaning for the motel, plus short order cook, plus baking, and dishes. One day I had my hands into a huge bowl of pastry, (I made all my own pies) and Bud was 'supposed' to be serving the customers. I heard a voice saying, "Hey, does anyone work here?" To which I pulled my doughy hands out of the bowl and went in search of Bud. I went to the washrooms and even outside. No Bud. So I washed my hands, and went and got their order and went back to the kitchen to cook it. As I was serving the meal, I happened to look out the front of the restaurant's window and here Bud was on a Grey Coach Bus waving goodbye! I nearly flipped. I don't think my mouth stopped flopping for a month after that one!

CAR BUYING

Then there were the 'good deals' he bought either at an auction (car or otherwise) and through the Penny Saver Newspaper. He would scan the newspaper, and up the stairs he would come from his smoking room with an itsy-bitsy piece of paper that he had torn out. He would inform me that this was 'THE' deal of a lifetime! It would be some old car or piece of junk. He would hound and hound then he would promise me that he would quit smoking if I only would let him have that deal of a lifetime. I would give in and go with him to 'just look at it'. Just a look! He had said. When we got there, of course, it was 'exactly' what he had been looking for. He put a deposit down on it, a big deposit in case someone else came in with a higher deposit. We were to pick it up the next day. But, in the meantime, he scanned the paper again, and found yet another one, a better deal than the other. We had to go and look at it, as we still had not finalized the other (although we had placed a hefty deposit down) and this new one was way better than the one he placed a deposit on. I said, "Well, what about the one you put a deposit on?"

"Oh, Gail, never mind that one. This is better."

"But," I said, "We put a deposit on the other."

"Never mind, this is what I was looking for."

With that, we brought the last one home, just in case someone else would come and buy it. He drove it home, no insurance, no license, and no nothing! It sat in the driveway all night. The next morning there was a puddle of oil running down the driveway. No comment!

PLANET HOLLYWOOD

I recall the time Bud bought an old truck from a guy. When Bud got it home, he was cleaning it out and found a real good pair of jogging pants with matching sweatshirt, from Planet Hollywood. Bud thought it great! He had me shorten the legs, (like a good foot) and shorten the sleeves, (like a good foot) of the sweatshirt. The next day he was donning his new attire, strutting around like a peacock. Our doorbell rang, and it was the man that sold him the truck and he wanted to talk with Bud. Bud, unaware what the man wanted, met him out in the garage. Here Bud is standing with this man's outfit on, much shortened, and the man came in search of the outfit. He said he had put it behind the seat of the truck and forgot it. He said he got it at Planet Hollywood and he wanted it back. Bud stood there, afraid to turn around because there was a big logo with the wording, 'Planet Hollywood'. Bud told him he never saw it.

MEXICO TRIPS

Then there were the times of our trips to All Inclusive places far away. I would tell him to not drink the water, unless it was bottled, especially while in Mexico. Well, of course, what harm can water do? I recall one such memorable time that we were on the plane flying home to Toronto. Just as the Captain announced that we would be soon touching down in Toronto, everyone decided to make that time, their bathroom time. I got up and stood in the very long line-up waiting for one of the four bathrooms at the back of the plane. I had asked Bud if he needed to go. No, he was fine. While I was standing in line, I felt a tap on my shoulder and it was Bud asking to take my spot in line. Well, long after I was back in my seat, Bud had not come out of the bathroom. The announcement came over the speakers that everyone should return to their seat and buckle up. No Bud. Eventually he arrived. He didn't want to sit down, he preferred to stand, he said. But he was soon ushered to take his seat. He quietly informed me that he had a problem. A big problem. He had to remove his undershorts and didn't know what to do with them so he tucked them into the napkin holder. He informed me too, that he had to take off his socks, and use them, as he had used up all the paper towels and toilet paper in the washroom. He said he wasn't in good shape. And he said that the bathroom was unfit for any others needing it. No more about that subject.

MEMORY LANE

Then there was the time we took a trip up north. Down memory lane we called it. There was a boil water notice up at all the Provincial Parks up north. "Come on, Gail! How can well water be bad? That is an old sign," he said, as he wolfed down a few cups of nice cold water.

Well, we had a little Boler trailer at the time. You know, those little ones that there is only one bed, and not much else. During the night he had the urge to go to the washroom, fast. The washroom was perhaps about 10 units away, but must have seemed like 100 miles to him. He said he couldn't make it and besides it was dark out and he couldn't see. He decided to just let out a little to relieve the pressure as he perched his behind over the park bench. When he informed me what he had done, I told him as soon as the first light of the sun peers over the horizon, he had better get his behind out there and clean up things, as we had a little dog and I couldn't put her out if there was any mess. Well, as soon as it was light, out he went, he came back and told me that he couldn't find it, and suggested that perhaps some wild animal might have come around.

The little Boler trailer that we were hauling had no springs, therefore, when travelling, everything, and I mean EVERYTHING bounced around and landed on the floor.

We stopped to have a rest, and when I opened the door of the trailer, what met my eyes was a jar of peanut butter, bottle of oil, bottle of vinegar and a bottle of jam all emptied, their lids had popped off and the mixture ran out of the cupboards and down the walls, all over the stove, micro-wave and eventually its final resting place was all over the floor. I only had a very small bottle of drinking water and a roll of paper towels to clean the mess up with. Bud took one look and grabbed a chair and took off to the bush to keep out of my hair and out of range of my mouth!

It was so bad that I had to tear up all the carpet and leave the remnants of the disaster until we got somewhere that there was hot water, and lots of it.

QUITTING SMOKING...AGAIN

There was the time we bought a farm. A hobby farm. It was way out of the city and Bud was afraid he wouldn't be able to get to the store to buy cigarettes like he did in the city. So for nearly a year, he would buy on the side a package of cigarettes when he filled up with gas. We moved to the farm and my sister came to visit us. Of course she had to see everything, including the barn. While he was showing her the barn, I happened to notice some green sticking out of the hay that was piled over in one side of the barn. I sent my sister in with Bud to see other areas of the barn, while I grabbed a huge garbage bag and filled it to nearly the brim with packages of cigarettes. That night, my sister and I watched as Bud made his way to the barn. He was out there for hours. We watched as the lantern made its way from window to window. He came back in the house and never said a word. I would hand him out one package a day for months on end. I overheard him telling a neighbour one day, "Imagine, she is handing out my own cigarettes."

TEXAS

There was a time when we were coming home to Ontario after spending 6 mths. in Texas. It was getting dark and we had to start looking for a place to spend the night. We drove into one on State Parks, which were open, but not manned yet. We were the only ones in a park that must have held perhaps 500 units. We drove around and around, looking for the 'perfect' spot. Eventually we came across one that was 'it'. We settled in for the night and the next morning we let our little dog out for her morning bathroom break. When she came back in, she smelt terrible, like, manure. We looked out and here we parked in the area where they put the horses for riding. There had to be mounds and mounds of the stuff. Of all the camping sites, we happened to pick that one!

Then there are the stories of the days when we owned a Hotel up north, way up north.
I won't go into them here in this book.

ANOTHER MEXICO STORY

I recall one of our Mexico trips. We were the only ones in this Park. I was making breakfast, and I saw three men approaching us. Two went to where Bud was sitting smoking, and the other came around the back and to the side door. I had our little dog with me, and the man at the door sweet talked our dog out and into his arms.

The other two men asked Bud for a cigarette in broken English, and Bud and the two men started into a deep conversation, them in Spanish and Bud in English. I said to Bud, "Bud, I think we should get out of here, fast."

"It's okay. I have it all under control."

"Bud, we have to leave, NOW!" I over emphasized.

"Hey, they guys understand me, and I understand them, isn't that something?"

"Bud, we have to leave, NOW!" again I spoke out loudly, perhaps I was yelling by now.

Bud realized what might be going on, only after the third man was now inside the motor home with me and the dog!

Bud started the Motor Home up and the man inside jumped out.

TREADMILL

Then I recall I was on the treadmill down in the rec. room. He was on the couch. The news was on. It happen to mention about a baby being washed up on shore. I was horrified and I spoke out, loudly, "My goodness, a baby washed up on shore!"

His reply, "How can a baby walk on shore?"

"I said, a baby washed up on shore!"

"I heard you! How can a baby walk on shore?"

I think I repeated the same sentence a few more times, and his reply the same, when I flew off the treadmill and over to his ear and yelled, "I said! The baby washed, washed, washed, and washed up on shore!!!"

"You don't need to shout."

HOUSE SMELL

We had a hobby farm one time. The house was well over 100 years old. There was an odd smell we noticed, only when the wind came from the north/west. I suggested that perhaps maybe one of the vents on the roof for the toilets may be plugged. So, Bud got up there with the garden hose, and ran water down the one. I went in the house, and it 'appeared' that the smell was gone. I went out and yelled that the smell was gone. He came down, hose and all.

The next day, the smell was back. Up on the roof he went again, hose and all. Again he put water down the vent, for the other toilet.

The next day, the smell was back.

I suggested that maybe the line going to the septic could be leaking under the floor of the old house. As I mentioned the house was well over 100 years old, and the beams under the floors were huge. Bud lifted the carpet and chopped into the floor, only to run into a beam. He moved over a few feet and chopped again in to the floor, another beam. I think he chopped maybe 5 times before we found a small area that I could crawl down through to take a look. He was to go upstairs and flush the toilets, while I remained down in the crawl space that neither man nor beast had ever been in for a hundred years. I happened to see something out of the corner of my eye and there a huge white snake that looked like a rattler, looking at me! I flew out of the hole and when he came down to see if I noticed any leakage, I told him what had happened.

He then peered down into the hole, and sure enough, he saw it too. We covered up the hole, nailed it shut, and covered all the areas again with the carpet. We then went to the walls. Chop, chop, and chop. We found the source of the smell. The sink up stairs was leaking down behind the wall. Someone put in a new line, but did not close off the old one. The snake? We believed it to be a milk snake, so someone said.

THE OLD TELEVISION

There was the time Bud saw an old Television in the garbage up the street. It was winter time and it has sat out for days, covered in snow. Bud hauled it home. My dad and mom were visiting and Bud comes in with this television. He wipes all the snow off and starts to plug it in. My dad was horrified and said, "You aren't going to plug that in, are you?"

"Sure why not?" he asked as he plugged it in. Sparks flew, it sizzled and sparked. But, the picture came on and much to my dad's amazement, it worked for years!

SEWING MACHINE

Another of Bud's pick-ups from the garbage. One day I wanted to go to the Mall. He suggested he could drive me. But, he had to do his 'garbage run' as he called it. He happened to notice a sewing machine, and he stopped the car. I was embarrassed, as I knew a lot of people in the city, so hid down on the floor in the car while he was rummaging. He packed the sewing machine in the trunk, then a lady hollered, "Here, do you want the electric cord, too?"

~~

UTILITY SHED FROM A GRAVEYARD

We had a lot up on the Nottawasaga River. We only had a tent on it. Bud saw a notice of a shed for free that was in a graveyard in Toronto. It had to be moved. So, on a Sunday morning, with an old car, and an older trailer, with a spare tire that was bald as was the other tires on it. We got nearly out of Toronto when we had a flat. We got that changed, and continued. We were pulled over by the Police as the shed was over-width and over-height. Bud said he was bringing it to an old lady up on the next concession road. He let us go.

We continued on our journey and were then pulled over by the Department of Transport. It just so happened that same old lady that lived just north of Toronto must have moved. So we got a warning that he better not see us up the road further.

We got on the main highway, 27, and we came to an overpass. We came down the dip, and then the top of the shed got stuck on the overpass. I did mention this was Sunday morning didn't I? Well, traffic started getting heavier, and now there was a lineup of cars behind us and in front of us as they couldn't get through as the shed was too wide.

Bud suggested that I stand out on the side of the hill and direct traffic, as he tried his best to back up.

We did get out of that mess without the Department of Transport of Police coming, and we got to the bridge that we had to pass over to get to our lot. It was Spring-time and the bridge had washed out. We couldn't get across. Bud went to a farmer and got the farmer to take us through the river with the trailer and shed.

We never used that shed for anything other than a toy box for our son!

BASEBALL CAP

Bud loved wearing baseball caps with a nice logo on it. And, he loved only caps that had that 'nice bend' to it. We were at Church one Sunday, and in their Gift shop he noticed baseball caps. He loved the shape and bought one without looking at the logo. He could hardly wait until we left Church so that he could slap it on his head. When we got out, he donned his cap. I looked at the motif and it read, "Jesus Saves'. I mentioned it to him and he said, 'Oh, I thought it said something else." And with that, the cap sat on the shelf in his closet never to be worn.

CHURCH

We used to go to a little Church in Prince Edward Island, which held about 60 parishioners. As you all might have guessed, he was deaf, and had to wear hearing aids, and even with them in, he had to speak very loud so that he could hear what he was saying. One such time, while the minister was speaking, he leaned over to me and shouted, "Is she good?" And another, "Is she finished, yet?" And another, "Good. One more hymn and we can go." And another, "I guess they have the slits in the sides of their gowns so that they can reach in and pull their pants up."

I cannot begin to count the times Bud would have a cigarette hanging out of his mouth while he filled the lawn motor with gas, or smoking while doing something with propane.

He has since passed away, but every time we hear a huge blast of thunder, we all think it is Bud up there causing some sort of explosion.

CPSIA information can be obtained at www.ICGtesting.com
Printed in the USA
LVOW06s0349091215

465966LV00001B/70/P